The Life and Times of Lilly the Lash™

The Toy Store
Written By Julie Woik

To Bethune Library—

Share the love of reading with everyone you meet!!

WAHOOOOO

November 2011

Snow in Sarasota Publishing, Inc.
Osprey, FL 34229
Library of Congress Cataloging in Publication Data
Woik Julie
The Toy Store
(Book #2 in The Life and Times of Lilly the Lash™ series)

p. cm.
ISBN – 978-0-9663335-8-9
1. Fiction, Juvenile 2. Psychology, self-esteem 3. Multi-cultural

First Edition
10 9 8 7 6 5 4 3 2 1

Design: Elsa K. Holderness
Illustration: Marc Tobin

Printed by Arcade Lithographing, Sarasota, Florida
in the United States of America

ABOUT THIS BOOK

The Life and Times of Lilly the Lash™ is a series of fascinating children's books, in which an **EYELASH** teaches life lessons and the importance of strong self-esteem.

Adventurous, yet meaningful storylines told in rhythm and rhyme, accompanied by spectacular cinematic-like illustrations, provide the tomboyish main character with a marvelous opportunity to teach children valuable lessons, while entertaining at every turn.

These whimsical tales for boys and girls age 0 – 10 (to 110!), will break their world of imagination wide open, and transcend their hearts and souls beyond their wildest dreams.

In book two of the series, *The Toy Store*, Lilly the Lash finds herself in New York City, where a young boy's access to every toy imaginable, leaves him feeling saddened and alone, due to his inability to create friendships through the value of **SHARING**. Lilly, only ever seen by the reader, sends in a loving, soulful child to help him recognize that sharing is part of what makes every experience in life so worth living.

LEARNING ACTIVITIES

Be sure to check out Lilly's website **www.lillythelash.com** to find the array of **FREE** Lesson Plans, Crafting Activities, and Games created for various age ranges and multiple learning levels. These amazing activities are designed for the educational community in a classroom setting, as well as the family structure in a home environment.

Laughing, Loving, and Learning
Hmmmm…Lilly might just have something here!

DEDICATION

To Roger
It's really quite odd you know,
you've seemed to come into our home
at a time when I needed to practice what I preach
...the art of genuine SHARING.
All a part of Lilly's clever planning I suspect!

Your loving friend,
Julie

THE TOY STORE

Book #2 in the Series
The Life and Times of Lilly the Lash™

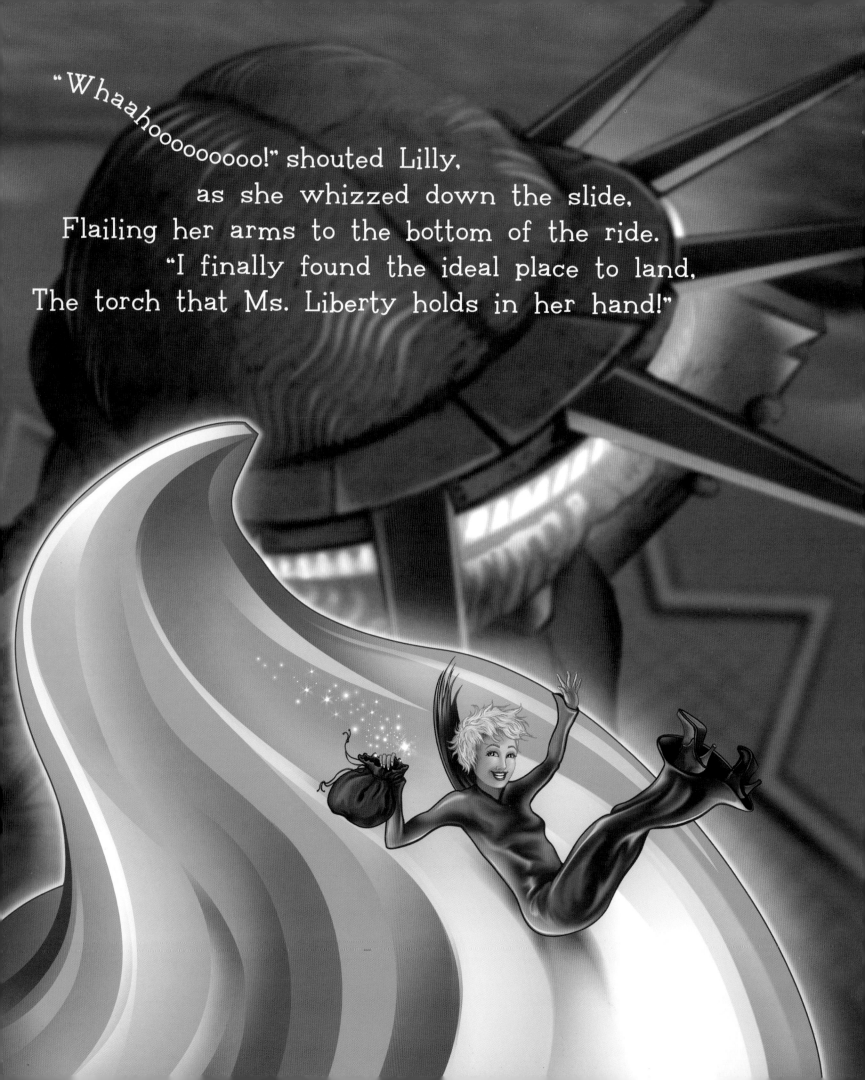

"Whaahoooooooo!" shouted Lilly,
as she whizzed down the slide,
Flailing her arms to the bottom of the ride.
"I finally found the ideal place to land,
The torch that Ms. Liberty holds in her hand!"

A jump to her feet, Lilly checked the brochure.
Tomorrow she'd plan for a city wide tour.
Observing the sights and the sounds for a trace,
Hoping they'd lead her to just the right place.

The night would creep in changing buildings and cars,
To a dazzling spectrum of diamond-like stars.
This place was alive with a heart and a soul,
The perfect location for Lilly's next goal.

Bursting with color, the sun filled the sky.
A beautiful day for Ms. Lilly to fly.
On her way into town, she was simply amazed,
By the volume of people, unique in their ways.

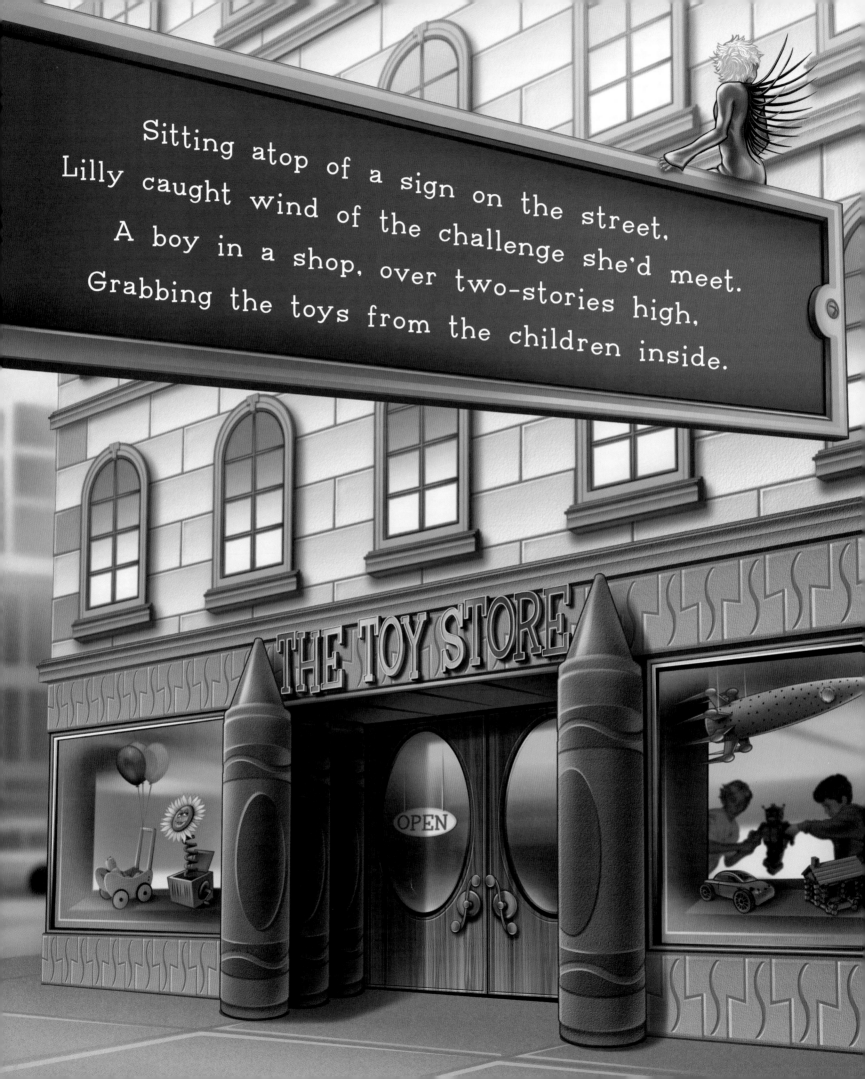

Sitting atop of a sign on the street,
Lilly caught wind of the challenge she'd meet.
A boy in a shop, over two-stories high,
Grabbing the toys from the children inside.

With shoulders hung low and a frown on his face,
He quickly stomped off to his favorite place.
"These are all mine," Tommy yelled from the floor,
"'Cause my Mom and Dad own the things in this store."

Completely aware of the task soon to come,
  Lilly flew straight, for the shelf, with the drum.
Landing off balance, she let out a scream,
  As the sticks began rolling like logs in a stream.

Just when these musical tools came to rest,
Lilly hopped down, as she patted her chest.
"That was a giggle," she said with a sigh,
"But I'd better take notes for the next time I fly!"

This Lilly I speak of, it's time you should know,
Once lived as my eyelash a long time ago.
Perched on my eyelid, she showed me the way,
To seek out the treasures that filled each new day.

A precious young spirit you couldn't ignore,
She'd ask me to see, what I'd not seen before.

"You may have not noticed," she'd say with a smile,
"But the world spins around every once in a while."

Changing Times

FOR THE PEOPLE

☀ Sunny 68

The World Around Us

Did you ever stop and think about
the things you do, and how they may
affect the world around you? As time
quickly moves before our eyes, it's
more important than ever for us to
recognize that we're all part of a big
beautiful picture.

Our actions and deeds, no matter
their size, affect the universe as a
whole. Be part of it today!

Hottest Children's Book Series

The Life and Times of Lilly the Lash

Everyone's crazy
fascinating, these
sweeping the country,
EYELASH who teaches
and life lessons, these
give your children
adventure, while
values
www.lillythelash.com

She'd always make things seem so simple and clear,
I found my soul listening when Lilly was near.
"When you give of yourself, you get twice the return."

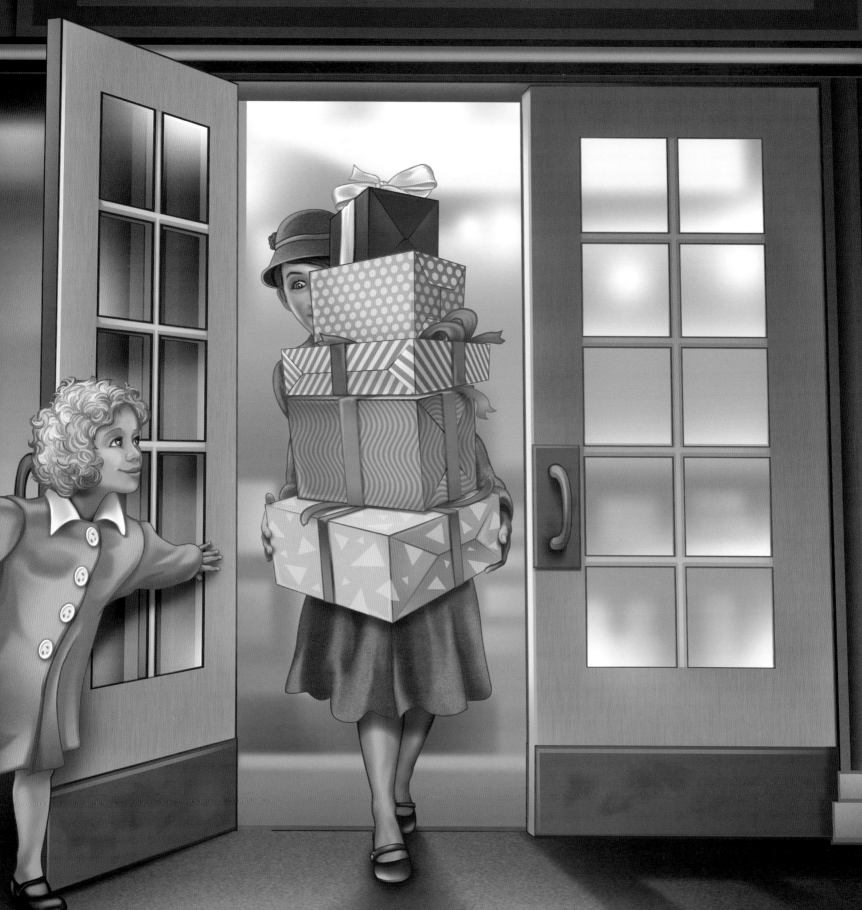

"And your heart," she would say, "holds the gold that you earn."

Being kind
is the kind of thing
to be

But soon I'd discover not everything lasts,
That the future, in time, becomes part of the past.
Lilly would have other journeys to take,
To pass on these values for everyone's sake.

A quick forty winks and off she would be,
Her satchel in hand, and a picture of me.
In the blink of an eye she was gone like a flash,
To start the adventures of Lilly the Lash.

So now let's return to the tale being told,
Where the message of sharing begins to unfold.
A crow's nest set high, like a ship's royal throne,
Was the sight Lilly chose, for her new wooden home.

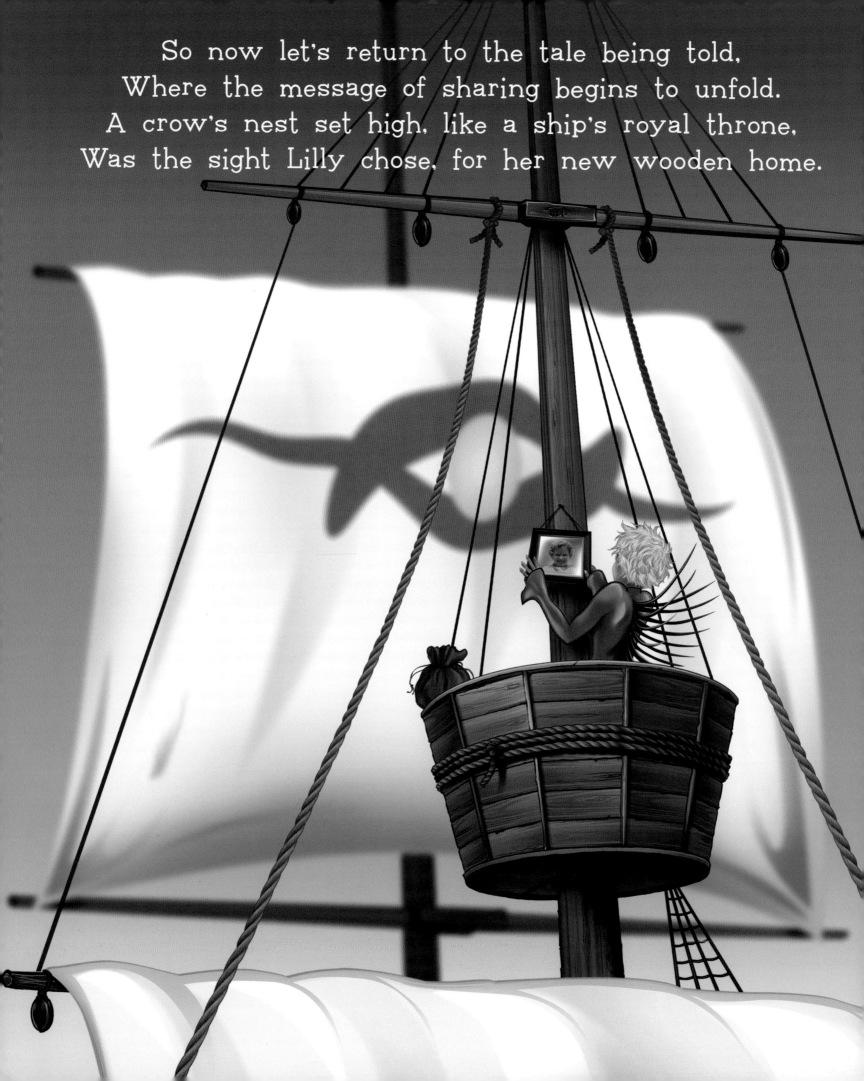

"I'm sad to see Tommy
behave as he does,
Collecting these things
that he 'thinks' that he loves."

"He must start to see," Lilly thought to herself,
"That it's FRIENDSHIP that brings you true fortune and wealth."

"Hey Max, kick it high!" you could hear someone shout.
Then Oliver ducked and yelled, "Mummy, look out."
As Ruth looked at Shaun with a smile ear to ear,
Her voice softly spoke,

"These are your sons,
my dear."

Filled with delight
from their heads to their toes,
The lads carried on
without worry or woe.
And when Mickey and Pierce
wanted in on the fun,
They made room on the team,
to include everyone.

Tommy, alone, with his nose to the glass,
Watched the boys in the park kick a can in the grass.
He could not understand, how without a new toy,
They were laughing and running and jumping with joy.

Like a statue he stood, just as still as could be,
Then his eye caught a glimpse of the Candy Stick Tree.
Beneath all the treats that hung high off the ground,
Sat two little girls, with a game they had found.

Carefully opening the sample display,
They set up the pieces and started to play.

"I love Secret Satchel," said Haley to Kate,
"A bag full of lessons that makes you feel great."

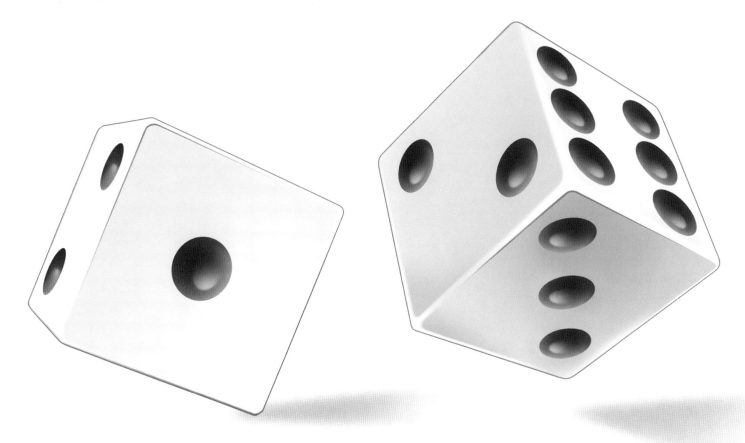

Just as the dice took its very first roll,
Tommy appeared and then lost all control.
Foolishly screaming out silly demands,
And yanking the cards that they held in their hands.

The girls now frightened, ran straight down the hall,
But didn't quite know what to make of it all.
As they turned, they saw Tommy, standing next to the train,
With his hands in his pockets, and his face full of pain.

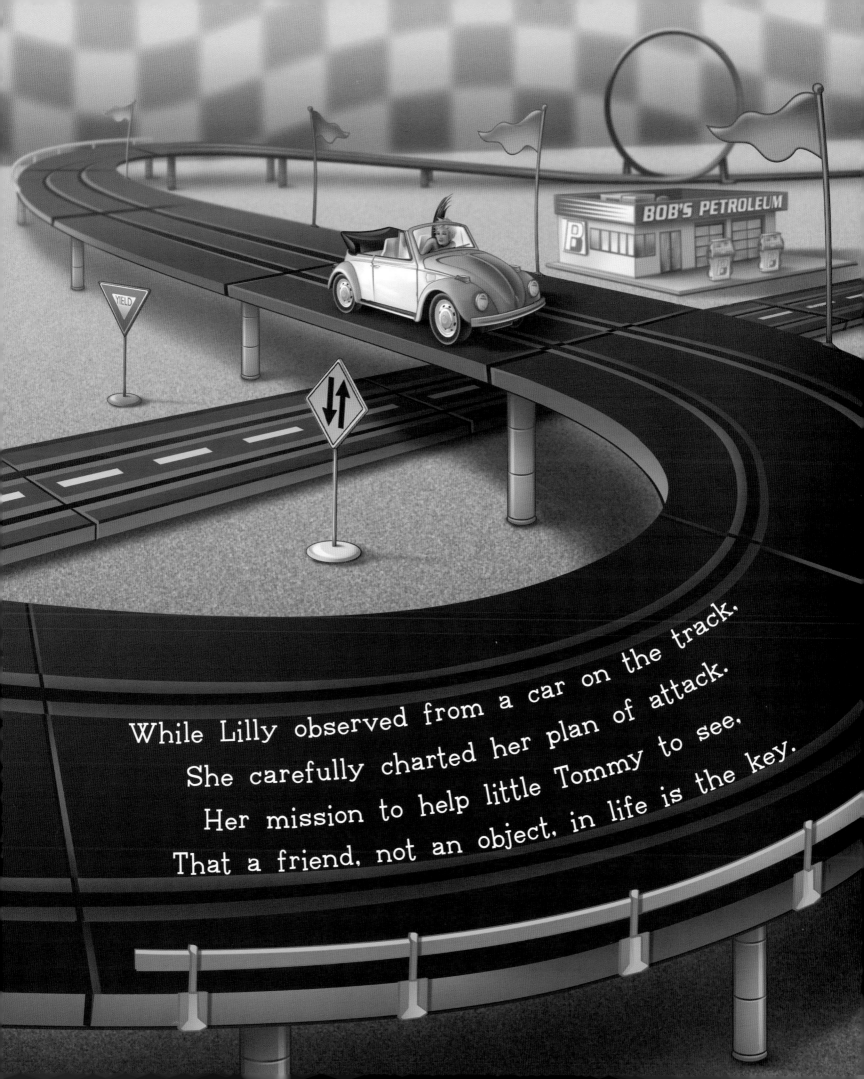

While Lilly observed from a car on the track,
She carefully charted her plan of attack.
Her mission to help little Tommy to see,
That a friend, not an object, in life is the key.

Scribbling it down just as fast as she could,
She had figured a way to teach Tommy some good.
With a satisfied look, Lilly hugged the first turn,
As she set into motion, the process to learn.

Macaulay and Aaron strolled in the front door. Overwhelmed by the sights, they set off to explore.

From the stairs, Aaron hollered, "Better watch out below!"

Then he swiftly slid down on the firemen's pole.

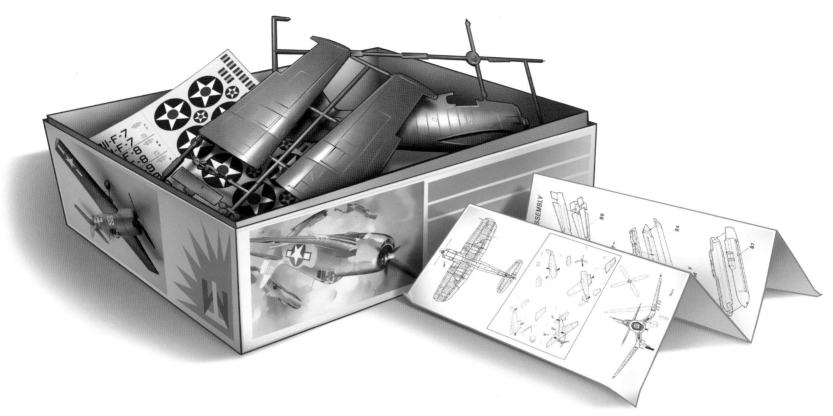

Upon Aaron's landing, he saw the remains,
Of a kit that was used to build large model planes.

As Macaulay walked over to pick up the box,
Tommy sprung from behind a huge pile of blocks.

"What da ya think you're doin' over there? These are alla my toys, and I don't like to share."

It took a brief moment, then scratching his head, Aaron kindly asked Tommy, "Did you mean what you said?"

A bit taken back, Tommy never had heard,
A caring response when his outbursts occurred.
Staring down at his shoes, he quite sadly confessed,
"I act in this way, then I feel so depressed."

With a kindhearted gesture that truly was grand,
Aaron reached out to Tommy, and offered his hand.

"I think what you need is to meet a good friend,
Who will stand by your side from the start to the end."

Just in that second, time stopped for a rest,
So Ms. Lilly could do, what Ms. Lilly does best.
With her pouch full of magic, she loosened the rope,
Unleashing spectacular crystals of hope.

These luminous speckles
were made from ideals,
To be showered on those
who were longing to heal.

Offering more than
a light in the sky,
A new lash to guide them,
would spring from their eye.

Suddenly Tommy felt something quite strange,
A real sense of goodness, that brought on a change.
"It's not the possessions that make you feel whole,
But the lives that you touch, that brings peace to your soul."

From the dollhouse front step,
Lilly watched the kids play,
As her worries for Tommy
now drifted away.

She was already thinking
of where she would go,
If you see her around,
tell her I said "Hello!"

The End

. . . are you sure?

FUN FACTS

 The Statue of Liberty's torch was once a navigational aid to ships entering the New York harbor. In the mid-1980's, after years of corrosion, a new copper torch coated with gold leaf for protection, was constructed.

 Breathtaking structures that have graced the New York City skyline include the Empire State Building, the Chrysler Building, and the Twin Towers of the World Trade Center. Although the Twin Towers are no longer standing, they shall forever be in our hearts and minds!

 Drums have been traced back to ancient times. In Africa, drums were often used as speech. A pattern of beats played in a certain way could communicate vast amounts of information. Cool huh?

 A crow's nest is a structure in the upper part of the mainmast of a ship, that's used as a lookout point. In early ships it was simply a barrel or basket lashed to the tallest mast. Imagine that?!

 Kick The Can is a game that involves a can, someone to be "it", and hiding. The object of the game is for the person hiding to kick the can before the person who's "it" steps on the can and describes the hider's location. Check it out for yourself!

 Candy Sticks are made from sugar cooked in water, along with added flavors and ingredients. Hard candies like sticks and drops were available in the 1650's, however, they were costly and considered luxury items.

 A board game generally has two types of play. One is strategy, where you block or capture your opponent. The other is racing, where you begin at one point and hurry to the end. Sometimes it's a combination of both!

 When electric toy trains first appeared, they quickly gained popularity and grew in sophistication. They were often equipped with lighting, the ability to change direction, and even emit a whistling sound. Toot toooot!!

 The history of dollhouses dates back about 400 years. Once referred to as "baby houses", these displays were specifically designed for adults. Unlike the dollhouses of today, they were completely off limits to children. Weird, huh?!?

Lilly's headin' Down Under
(To the ocean floor that is!)

The Life and Times of Lilly the Lash
Ocean Commotion

While soaring the skies, Lilly hoped she would find,
The most beautiful place to relax and unwind.
As she peered through the clouds, Lilly's wish had come true,
"A paradise," she said, "with a marvelous view."

A miscalculation to land on the ledge,
Left Lilly one handed just over the edge.
"I may need more practice on landing in flight,
'Cause I think I'd have fallen, if my grip wasn't tight!"

From the Cà d'Zan tower overlooking the bay,
Came a prism of light slowly drifting her way.
The rippling waves washed a bottle ashore,
With a message that read, ***"WE'VE GOT TROUBLE GALORE!"***

(Watch for Book #3 in this Series)

Follow Lilly on her next adventure to
Rockin' Reef
Where a young octopus learns the important
Life Lesson of
HONESTY

SPECIAL THANKS

To Marc - The Illustrator
Well you know, you've done it again.
First of all, you make me laugh until I nearly cry.
Then you go and create images that not only
dazzle one's eye, but are totally ingenious as well.
And now you've become more than just Lilly's illustrator,
...you are my friend.
Thank you!

To Elsa - The Designer
Every single day you're there for me.
No matter if it's some new fangled idea I've come up with
to help children learn from Lilly and her books,
or whether I just need to giggle in an out of control kind of manner.
You're always standing right there, right by my side.
We've got so much to look forward to Elsa.
And the cool thing is, we get to do it together! Yahoooooooooo!!!!!!

To Kevin - Snow in Sarasota Publishing
What a lovely person you are. So reassuring.
Always there with endless support and such kind words.
You've lifted my spirits on days when I've needed it most.
You understand the experience, and you've got a
certain way of making everything feel okay.
You're very special.

To The Kids
I'd like to thank all of the children who were part of this book.
Oliver, Max, Pierce, Mickey, Haley, Saischia (aka Kate), and Macaulay.
A special thanks goes to Jacob (aka Tommy) for selflessly allowing
me to use him as an example, so others could learn about sharing.
And to Aaron, who in life, is always there to offer his hand.
This is our future. What a spectacular group!

To My Treasured Parents
People ask me every day how Lilly the Lash came to be.
The real truth of it is, Lilly came to be because I've had the
most wonderful upbringing anyone could ever ask for.
Because of you, Mom and Dad, I'm happy. Truly happy.
Lilly came from a place so loved, that she wanted everyone
in the whole wide world to feel that exact same love.
Thank you for giving Lilly life!

Making Our World A Better Place

A percentage of the profit from this book will go to the:

National Lung Cancer Partnership
RESEARCH. AWARENESS. CHANGE.

In Memory of our friend
Shaun Roy Hunter

You have moved on, yet we remain.
But before you went, you created two beautiful children
for all of us to love and laugh and grow with.

…until we meet again
Love, Julie